W9-BIX-681

Copyright © 2014 by Emma Yarlett

All rights reserved. No part of this book may be reproduced, transmitted, or
stored in an information retrieval system in any form or by any means, graphic,
electronic, or mechanical, including photocopying, taping, and recording,
without prior written permission from the publisher.

First U.S. edition 2015

Library of Congress Catalog Card Number 2014939356
ISBN 978-0-7636-7595-0

TLF 19 18 17 16 15
10 9 8 7 6 5 4 3 2

Printed in Dongguan, Guangdong, China

This book was typeset in Book Antiqua.
The illustrations were created digitally.

Edited by Libby Hamilton
Designed by Mike Jolley

TEMPLAR BOOKS

an imprint of Candlewick Press
99 Dover Street
Somerville, Massachusetts 02144
www.candlewick.com

***Orion
AND THE
DARK.

templar books

an imprint of Candlewick Press

My name is **Orion,**
and I guess you could say
I am scared of a lot of things.

Mom tells me I just have
a big imagination and there's
nothing to be frightened of.

Well, that's easy for **her** to say.

As far as I can see, the world is **full** of frightening things.

But there is one thing that scares me more than anything else . . .

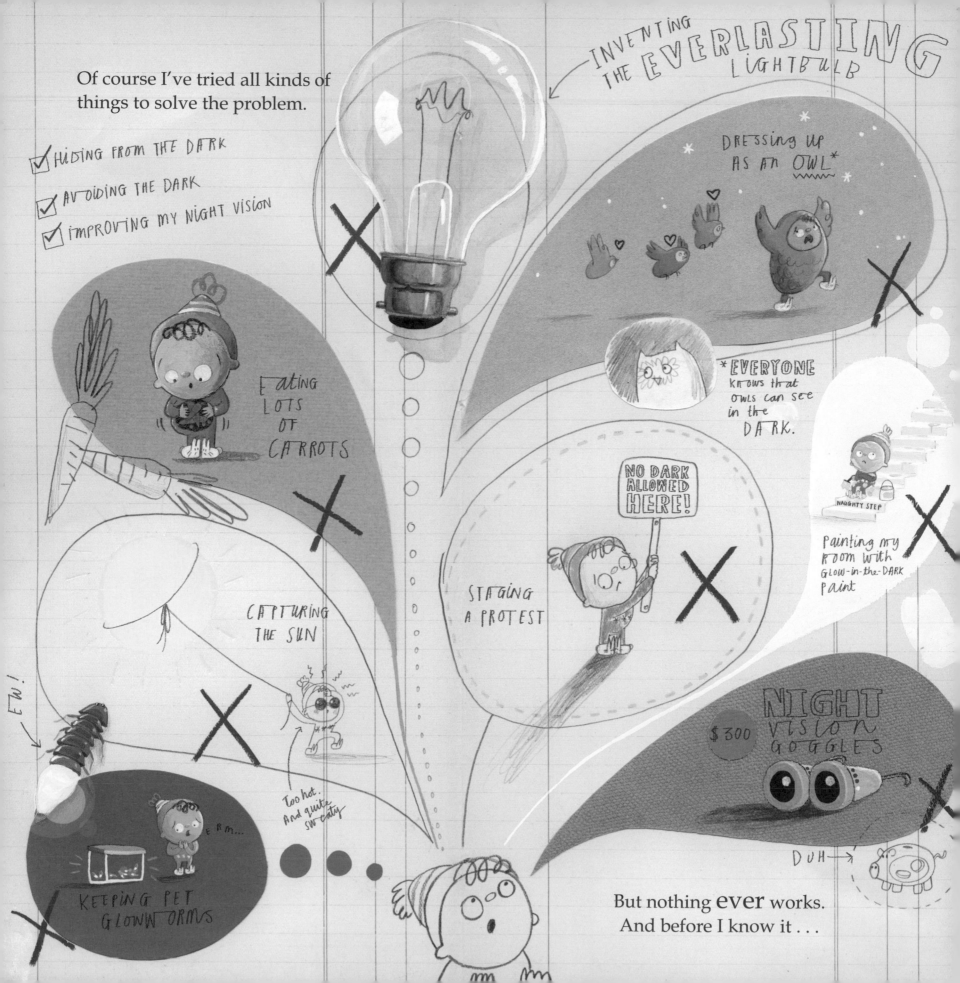

it's bedtime again.

I hate bedtime.

The night that changed everything began like any other.
I kept an eye out for monsters.
I kept an ear out for scary noises.

But as it got darker . . .

and darker . . .

and darker . . .

I couldn't take it anymore.

And that's when something strange happened.

Outside my window, the Dark seemed to come alive!

And then it came inside my room!

I was feeling more scared than **ever before.**
(Even more than when I went to that dog show with Grandma.)

But Mom always says it is important to remember your manners,
especially when you are greeting ~~monsters~~ visitors.

So I said,

Hello.
I'm ORION.***

And put out my hand.

Hello there.
I'm the **DARK**.
Now, Orion,
it's time for you to stop
being so afraid of everything.
Especially me!
Let's go on an
adventure.

Of course, **normally** I'd be scared stiff of going on an adventure,
especially with a terrifying creature like the Dark . . .

. . . but the Dark wasn't quite
what I had expected.

First he asked to see the **shadowy** and **scary** parts of the house,
the nooks and crannies where the **monsters** live.

1. In the CLOSET

2. UNDER the BED

3. Down the DRAIN

4. In the BASEMENT

And you won't believe this, but some
of the darkest places turned out to be . . .

ORION

BOUNCE

the most

FUN!

LOOK at
my RABBIT
SHadow!

Even having fun couldn't stop me from being scared for long, though.

The Dark asked me if I had stopped feeling afraid.

I said I felt a little better, but there was still one place that made my knees wobble and my tummy twist with **fright** . . .

And so off we went . . .

on one last adventure, all the way up into the **night sky.**

There, in the darkest place of all, I realized the Dark could be fun,

and the Dark could be interesting,

and the Dark could be magical.

And most of all . . .

the Dark could be my friend.
And nobody (not even me) is scared of their best friend.

But

too soon

we had

to go

home.

As the sun began to climb back up into the sky,
my friend began to fade. It was time to say good-bye.

I've had such a SUPER-DUPER, SPIFFADOCIOUS, INCREDAMUNDO ADVENTURE. But will you EVER come BACK?

And from that night on,

he never was.

I didn't want the Dark to go.

And so he promised,

I'll never be far away.

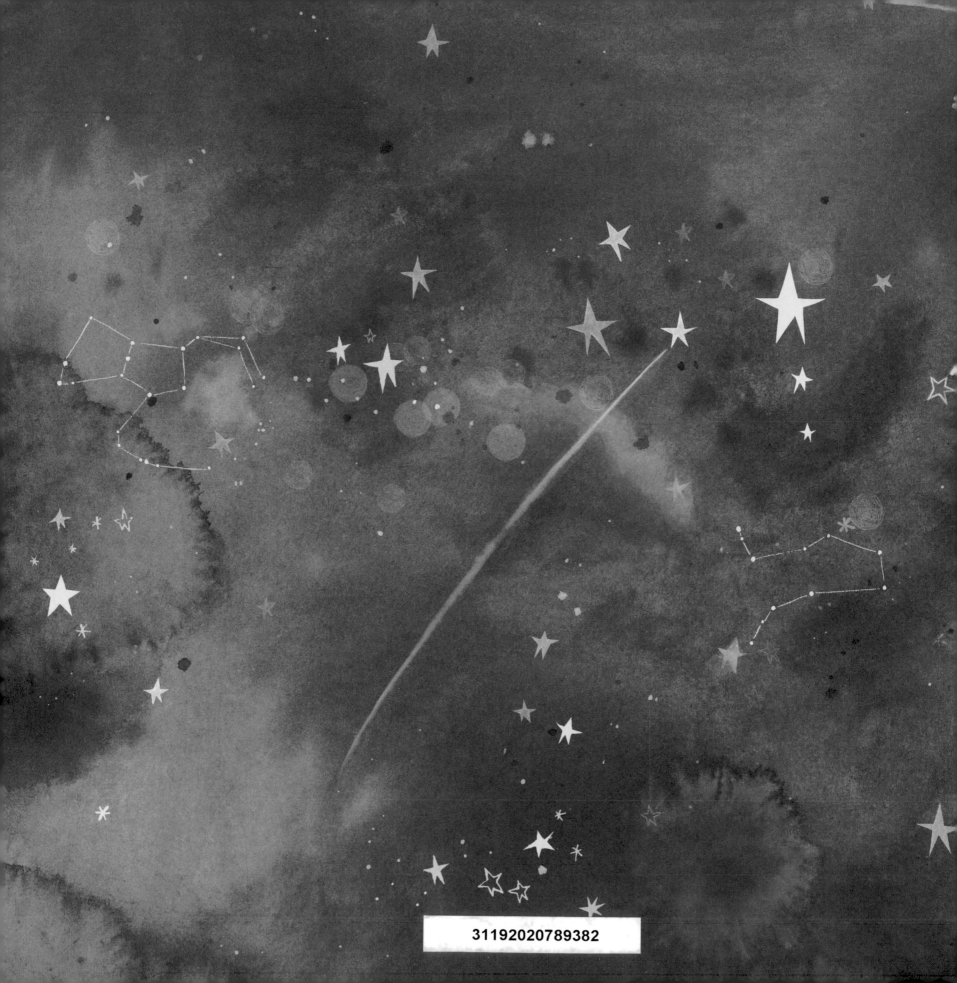

31192020789382